Dreams are

Everly Jones seems to have it all—a good job, a nice home, lots of friends, and a joyful spirit. If only everyone knew the torture she faced each night when she fell asleep. Everly inherited more than her house from her grandmother; she also inherited her ability to dream walk. Lately, she has spent her nights connecting with a young girl in terrible peril.

Hal Sims spent his career in the military finding people who were considered "unfindable," and when his career was cut short after losing vision in one eye, he sank into a routine of dead-end jobs and self-pity. Until The Phoenix Agency came calling. They need his innate ability to put pieces together when no one else can. For the first time, though, he might be on a case even he can't solve. Thankfully, he doesn't have to do it alone.

When Everly's dreams lead her to Hal and his mission, she knows it is up to them to save the girl, along with all the others the girl can lead them to.

Dangerous Dreams is USA Today bestselling author Dara Fraser's contribution to Desiree Holt's popular shared world The Phoenix Agency. It features a dream-walking heroine who never gives up fighting for those who need her, a smexy Phoenix Agency agent who doesn't allow his partial blindness to get in the way of completing his mission, and a little girl with a gift far too powerful to be left in the hands of evil.

Dangerous Dreams

ISBN: 978-1-68361-397-8

Print ISBN: 978-1-68361-401-2

Cover art by Fantasia Frog Designs

The Phoenix Agency

They served their country in every branch of the military – Army Delta Force, SEALs, Air Force, Marines. We are pilots, snipers, medics – whatever the job calls for. And now as private citizens they serve in other capacities, as private contractors training security for defense contractors, as black ops eradicating drug dealers, as trained operatives ferreting out traitors. With the women in their lives who each have a unique psychic ability, they are a force to be reckoned with. Risen from the ashes of war, they continue to fight the battle on all fronts. They are Phoenix.

Dear Reader,

Welcome to The Phoenix Agency, a covert and high concept security agency, whose partners have served their country in every branch of the military – Army Delta Force, SEALs, Air Force, Marines. Risen from the ashes of war, they continue to fight the battle on all fronts. They are Phoenix.

In this series you will read books by a multitude of fabulous, creative authors who will bring the world of adventure into your mind. Each story, is developed completely—plotting, writing, editing— by the individual authors, whose talent takes you into a world of vivid adventure. I am honored that they choose to be a part of this series.

Thank you for purchasing this book. I hope you will collect all of them.

Desiree Holt

P.S. I hope you will pick up the titles I have

written that established The Phoenix agency and its complex cast of characters: ***Jungle Inferno, Extrasensory, Scent of Danger, Freeze Frame, Feel the Heat, Formula For Danger,*** *and* ***Unexpected Risk.***

Dangerous Dreams
The Phoenix Agency

by

USA Today Bestselling Author

Dara Fraser

Chapter One

Everly

I began to hum the lullaby my grandmother sang to me all those years ago, the words no longer within my grasp. As softly and sweetly as I could, I used the only thing within my power to calm the sobbing child in my sight for as long as I remained there. The little girl couldn't see me, of that I was sure after spending the past couple of nights trying to bring her into my realm as she did the same to me from hers.

But sound? Sometimes…just sometimes, she heard me, and, by some miracle, it calmed her enough for the sobbing to stop. Maybe if she were a couple of years older, I'd be able to do more than hum, but at eight, possibly nine, whatever trace of ability she had that got me there was all she possessed.

So hum I did until the pull began, just as it had the previous two nights. The first night, I fought it so hard I woke up sore all over after my visit to the man's dreams. After that, I allowed myself to be dragged from this domain to his without hesitation. The girl and the man were connected. I didn't know how I knew that, but I did, and if visiting him meant I might be able to help her, I was going to do just that.

Closing my eyes, I continued to hum as I felt my body, such as it was, being transported. This time when I opened my eyes, I was sitting at a kitchen table, a tiny one at that, the entire surface covered with pieces of paper, all of them too blurry to read or make out. Across from me sat the man who'd brought me to him, although, based on all my attempts to communicate with him, I had a feeling he didn't know he was doing so, his gift most likely latent with the exception of me.

"There has to be something here." His fist came down on the table, the papers bouncing slightly with the motion then settling right back to their spots. He picked up a magnifying glass and bent closer to the table, and as he did so, certain pictures became clearer as if I were seeing them through his eyes.

Which really, this was his dream not mine. But what did that mean? Nothing had appeared blurry the other times I'd been in his dreamspace.

I pushed that thought to the side and concentrated

on the pictures he was now focused on. A family came into view, standing in front of a tree—a mom, a dad, and…*her*…the girl from my dream.

"Who is she?" I asked, but of course, he said nothing in reply. He couldn't hear me. His gift might possibly be strong given that he could reach me, but he didn't seem to know what to do with it, and I reckoned he didn't even know he was using it now.

I kept looking at the items piece by piece, trying to see what they all were, my presence fading with each passing moment. I needed to stay. There was something here I needed; something the little girl needed.

"Lucy, I will find you!" He slammed his fist down again then pushed himself up from the table.

Lucy. The little girl's name was Lucy. And she wasn't his daughter, not if the picture was telling the story I felt it was telling. No. He was someone else. But who and where was he? Maybe he was the one I needed to find.

Yes. That felt right. He was the key to finding Lucy.

"You're here again." He rubbed his eyes. "I can feel you. I promise you I am trying to find your little girl." No, he wasn't rubbing his eyes, he was wiping the tears I hadn't noticed forming. "I won't fail you."

I got up and walked around the room, not able to get far thanks to my ties to him. Who was he talking to?

"I know the answers are here. They have to be." He all but growled.

Someone knocked on his door, and, as he went to answer it, I saw for the first time he wasn't in his apartment. No. This was one of those long stay hotel rooms. But where?

He swung open the door, and two very drunk college-age kids almost fell in, immediately apologizing for pounding on the wrong door and stumbling off. The man did not respond to them, just shut the door and mumbled about how much he hated Mardis Gras.

Beep, beep, beep.

I felt myself being dragged away. There was no use fighting it. The beeping was my alarm, and I was powerless against waking up or at least coming out of my dream state. So, instead, I watched everything as I fell away, hoping for at least one more clue…something…anything.

And as I opened my eyes, all I wanted to do was scream at not being able to snatch even a crumb from the scene. Which made me more determined than ever to save Lucy.

Chapter Two

"You be good today." I petted Calvin's little head. "Catch any mouse who dares come in here but try not to scratch anything up."

There was no point to my speaking. He was the laziest cat ever when it came to mice, and he was going to keep clawing the one side table until the end of time, something he was very much not too lazy to do. But as long as he kept to the one piece of furniture, it wasn't as if I had much to complain about.

He purred in response to my gentle strokes, but I had to go or I'd be late to work. I grabbed my purse and headed to work. Thankfully, the traffic wasn't too horrible, and I managed to stop long enough to get a box of donuts for the office and still arrive on time. We were going to have a few meetings, and that was never any fun, so a donut bribe it was.

Where I really wanted to be was at home, sleeping so I could find out more information about Lucy. All I'd learned was the man was at Mardis Gras in

Louisiana and residing at a long term stay type hotel. It would have to be enough. This morning, I wasn't out of bed five minutes before I'd booked a trip to New Orleans for the weekend. If the flights for today hadn't been all booked, I'd have been on a plane, but honestly, what good would that do? I needed to figure out more.

And sleeping the day away wouldn't help unless they both were, too. So, work it was.

"Hey, boss." Martha grabbed the box of donuts from my hand. "No offense, boss, but you look pretty beat. Want me to make you one of my teas?" Martha was all into tea and made a concoction for every occasion, some of them were even yummy. Most tasted like dirt, but given they tended to work, I overlooked that part.

"That would be amazing. I didn't sleep well last night." Which was the problem with dream walking. It wasn't getting in a second day via the dream realm while getting a full eight hours of rest. Nope, it was like pulling an all-nighter most of the time. Grams said it would be different if I found someone my dreams naturally connected with. I'd asked her for clarification numerous times, but her response was that I would *understand when I understood.*

She said that one a lot, and I had to give it to her, for the most part, she was right. I understood about being tugged from dream to dream now that I had experienced it. I understood how to find someone again in the realm after doing so on accident one time. I understood how to block out all dream walking after a bout of the flu had me needing the sleep more than anything else.

But knowing understanding would come and having understanding when I wanted it were two very different things. I still found myself wishing I had pushed her for more information before she passed.

"I can see that. Maybe you can go home early tonight. Your schedule today consists of just the boring meetings you called." She winked at me and skipped off.

Maybe I should go home early. I could be packed for my trip and get some rest. Then maybe I'd be able to figure out what the man and Lucy were trying to tell me, something that would be hella easier if either of them knew they were reaching out to me.

I stepped into my office with an hour before the first meeting. It would be an easy one, no PowerPoint or handouts needed, just a *this is the exciting new thing we have on the horizon* type office pep rally of sorts. They were my favorite meetings. The others weren't run by me and would probably be mostly us pretending to listen as we pretended to take notes while corporate babbled on about the new "goals" which were always the same as the old ones except with new wording.

Which meant I had time to do a quick search. I turned on my laptop and googled for long term stay hotels in New Orleans. There were far more than I had anticipated, and I clicked on one after another, looking at their sample rooms. I'd managed to get through only five before Martha walked in with my tea.

"Whatcha doing?" She set down my mug, the scent of cinnamon tickling my nose. "Anything I can help with?"

"I was just looking at hotels in New Orleans. Thinking of taking a short holiday." *And saving a little girl who calls me into her dreams each night sobbing.*

"Wait until next month, trust me. You don't want to be stuck in Mardis Gras hell." She sat in the chair in front of my desk, a cup of tea in her hand as well. "When are you thinking of going?"

"This weekend." I watched as her eyes bugged out. "Figured I would leave Thursday after work."

"You want to go for Mardis Gras?" She gasped as if it were the most insane idea ever. Had I wanted to go for that reason, I'd have agreed with her. I was too old to be crammed in a street with a bunch of drunk strangers flashing boobs and who knew what else.

"I heard the king cakes are delicious."

"And they ship them now." She just shook her head at me. "Seriously though, if you can avoid this weekend, I would. Besides, tickets have to be insanely high right now." She was so not wrong there. I'd paid far more than I would under any other circumstance, but Grams always said, *What are you gonna do? Take it with you?* And could I live with myself if I didn't do everything within my power to help?

"My cousin, Ron, works at a nice hotel there.

Want me to call him for you?"

I had to give it to Martha, she might think I was crazy, but she was always willing to help me succeed in said crazy.

"Sure." I would need a place to stay, so why not? "Ugh, it's meeting time. Do you have the pom-poms ready?" I teased as I rose from my seat, my mission to find the mystery man needing to wait at least until after work.

"If by pom-poms you mean a nice tray of donuts, a fresh pot of coffee, and some really nice new pens, then yes, I have the pom-poms ready."

"Then let's get to this meeting and then maybe you and I could chat about me getting out of here early today and taking a nap or seven."

"Maybe a nap will help you see the insanity of attending Mardis Gras alone."

Except, I didn't plan to be there alone for long.

Chapter Three

"Calvin," I called as I entered my home. He came trotting over, caterwauling his strange *heh-row*. Such an odd cat. "Were you a good boy for Mama?" He rubbed against my leg. "I will pretend that is a yes." I bent down, picking him up and holding him close.

"Mama is pretty darn tired. You know dream walking is just as bad as staying awake all night." I scratched under his chin. "So, how about this? I will look up some more hotels and then you and I can take a nap?" I set him on the couch then grabbed my laptop and joined him.

Hotel after hotel and not one matched the picture plastered in my mind from my dream. But it had to be one of those hotels… I'd even seen one of those "save the whales and reuse a towel" plastic stands on the counter by the door.

My failure had me then searching for all places that celebrated Mardis Gras in case I was wrong on it being city specific, but everything I read told me New

Orleans was it. Which meant I was missing something. Of course, I was. And when my low battery notification popped on my screen, the amount of time I'd spent, absorbed into my research, hit me. So much for taking a nap.

"Dinner and bed, little fella." I shut the laptop and got up, stretching my back to release the stiffness from sitting hunched over the computer. When did I get so old?

I grabbed a frozen dinner and popped it in the microwave, Calvin circling his food bin the entire time. "I told you I'd get you your yums, silly boy."

I poured his food into his bowl then grabbed mine from the microwave, while mentally making a packing list. I still didn't know what I type situations I might run into and decided a little bit of everything was my best option—from leggings and a hoodie right on up to one of my nicer dresses. Reality was I would probably get there, wander around until my heart hurt because of my inability to find the man in my dreams or any clue about Lucy's whereabouts, and then head home. But just in case I hit the clue jackpot, I wanted to be prepared.

I threw my now empty dish into the trash and my fork into the sink. “Let’s go, Calvin. It’s time to pack.”

He was good about me leaving now, but when I first got him from the shelter, every business trip I took was an emotional disaster for the poor thing. All I had to do was bring out the suitcase and he was pacing.

“I sent a message to Christina, and she promises to take good care of you,” I reassured him, glad my neighbor loved my furbaby as much as I did. “Maybe I will even bring you back a present.” Not that he loved anything more than the ring around the milk cap.

An hour later, I was packed and ready for bed. It was earlier than I usually went to sleep, but some actual slumber before I started to go back to work looking for clues wouldn’t be a bad thing.

I breathed in.

One. Two. Three. Four. Five.

I held my breath.

One. Two. Three. Four. Five.

I exhaled.

One. Two. Three. Four. Five.

Repeat.

Repeat.

Repeat.

Next thing I knew, I was standing on a patch of grass, the sun so bright I needed to squint to take in my surroundings. In front of me stood Lucy wearing a fancy party dress, her hair longer than any of my previous dream walks, her cheeks rosy and full. This wasn't her showing me the present. Could she be showing me the past? Or was this her dreams of the future? With a skill as untuned as hers, it could be anything.

"Mom. Mom are you coming?" She called out, her hands cupped around her mouth.

"She'll be here in a bit, child." A man stepped out of the shade, wearing a big sun hat that had been out of fashion for decades—if it ever were truly in fashion. A pair of sunglasses shielded his eyes.

"Who are you?" Her voice quivered slightly as she took a step back. *Good girl. Always trust your gut.*

This man oozed sliminess.

"She told me to tell you she would be right out.

Said she had to call your father first to make sure he was ready with your birthday surprise." He didn't move, just stood there, his fake smile plastered across his face. His words must've appeased Lucy, for she relaxed slightly.

"She told you about the surprise?" Lucy tilted her head to the side.

He nodded. "She said you dreamed it."

"I'm not supposed to talk about that." Lucy slammed her mouth shut. So her parents did know about her gift. Then why was it so wonky? "Why would they tell you?"

"They said you saw a cute pony with a five on it."

"Three," she corrected then looked to the ground as if being caught doing something bad.

"Are you sure it wasn't a five? I could have sworn it was a five."

"*Mooooom!*" Lucy screamed at the top of his lungs.

The woman from the picture of the family, Lucy's family, came running outside, not looking at all shocked to see the man standing there.

"She's not ready. Make her ready." Was all he said as he strolled away.

"Mommy, what does he—"

"Shhh, Lucy. Don't worry about him." The woman was shaking slightly. "Let's get to your birthday surprise, shall we? Daddy found the pony you want, only it is wearing a number five, not a three. Will that do?"

And everything went black.

Chapter Four

Shut out from what I now knew was Lucy's memory, I found myself wandering in the dark. Normally, I'd allow myself to fall into a deeper slumber, but I was waiting for the mystery man to pull me in.

My ability allowed me to wander around on my own and pop into random dreams. That was a line I just wouldn't cross. Dreams were the one place people had complete privacy, and watching their deepest thoughts, the ones they often hid from even themselves, was an invasion I'd never intentionally do.

My grams had spent countless hours teaching me how to know the difference between an invitation and a person who just didn't have any walls up. A couple of times I erred in judgement as a teen, and I learned the hard way where those barriers were. It took me years to eat meat again after watching a particular hunter relishing in his kill, and while no part of me suspected his cruelty to be the norm, it still impacted my life greatly.

I found myself pacing in my dream state, unsure whether I should go looking for the man or wait until he yanked me into his space. Eventually, I lay down and allowed myself some real sleep, knowing that if he came calling, he had the power to get me where he wanted me to be.

He never came.

That didn't stop me from dreaming about him. Only my dream varied greatly from the ones he pulled me into night after night. In my dream, we were sitting at a table in a restaurant, a nice one at that, and the waiter had just brought us our dinner.

"Your eyes," he spoke wistfully, "they are so…amazing. Is that even the right words?"

I shrugged then hacked off a piece of my steak as if I weren't sitting across from not only the most attractive man I'd ever me, but also the one who had the answers to so many of my questions.

"I guess." I continued to cut my steak then found myself picking it up and swapping it out with his. What the heck? I wasn't his mother. "Steak at twelve."

And then everything clicked into place. He wasn't partially blind in my dream, he was mostly blind. Yet he was complimenting my eyes.

"Thanks, love." He reached down, brushed his fingers along the rim of the plate, then went to the left and picked up his fork. "I always did love this place."

"Only because we had our first date here." I scooped a green bean onto my fork. "Although if I recall correctly, you insisted it wasn't a date." My tone rang with amusement.

The dream was so bizarre. It was as if I was sitting outside of myself while being myself. I brushed the odd feeling away. I'd taken for granted that I had control over this dream, but maybe it was okay that I didn't.

It was probably a combination of letting myself get too worn down and not having enough REM sleep as of late.

"It wasn't. I was working." He pointed his fork in my direction to accentuate the point.

"If it wasn't a date, you wouldn't have bought me that beautiful dress," I countered. "No man buys a woman a fancy dress for a non-date. That's just ridiculous."

"I bought you the dress because you needed it." He shrugged. "But enough about that. When are you going to open your present?"

"Present?" I looked around then saw the small gift bag on the table.

"How quickly you forget. Maybe I should just keep it until our next anniversary." He chuckled, his voice deepening and oh so sexy.

"It's not our anniversary." Or was it?

"One year ago today was the first time I met you—or sort of met you." He put his fork down. "So present time."

I reached inside the small bag and found nothing. So I looked inside, only to see black that got bigger and bigger until I was no longer dreaming but, instead, waking up to the sound of my phone.

I grabbed it, mad at myself for not remembering to shut it down.

"Great," I moaned as the clock showed four a.m. Waking up an hour before you had to was the freaking worst.

The message was from Martha apologizing for being so early, and with her apology, she attached some pictures and asked me to call her.

Except they weren't *some* pictures, they were snapshots from her cousin's hotel and the room he had available last second. And it wasn't just *any* room. It was the one the man from my dream had been in that night.

I sprang up, startling Calvin who was asleep at my feet, and called her.

"Sorry to wake you, but my cousin said that they just had to kick out two drunk losers from this room, and he wanted to give you first option to it. Since it is Mardis Gras, he said, as soon as he clicks the official button to cancel, the rest of their reservation it will sell out. So, a four a.m. call it is." She always tended to babble when she was nervous, which she had no reason to be. She had given me what hours of searching for could not.

"Tell him I will take it. Do you have my information to give him?" I needed that room, I could feel it. That room was the key to finding both the man and the little girl.

"Nah, I'll give him your name and my card. Just switch it over when you get there. I'll give you all the info at work. Try to get some more sleep."

We hung up, and I put my head back on my pillow, but sleep would not come. Half an hour later, I got up and did the best thing I could think of, I bought a new ticket for New Orleans, this one leaving late morning. Work could wait. New Orleans no longer could.

Chapter Five

"It looks like we will be landing only a few minutes later than planned," the voice boomed over the intercom.

"I can't believe I'm here," the young man next to me said more to himself than me. "Mardis Gras."

I knew from our flight that he was meeting his friends there for a weekend of drunken craziness. He had far more plans than time, given his list of expectations for the few days he was spending in the city, though I ever mentioned that to him. His excitement saved me from hours on a plane with nothing to do except keep myself awake so as to not overshare my dreams with the entire plane. I had a tendency to say all of the words I spoke in the dream out loud for anyone nearby to hear, which was fine when the only one sharing my bed was Calvin. Far less fine whenever I attempted to start a relationship and had to make excuse after excuse as to why we couldn't sleep together even when we got naked together.

Not that I had bothered with that for far longer than I cared to think about. It was just too hard to hide things from a potential partner, and that was what I would have to do until, as Grams put it, *You know when it is time to share your secret.*

“Have a great weekend.” I grabbed on to the armrests as the wheels touched the ground, the landing somehow catching me unaware, even after we had a full-on announcement.

“You, too. What are you here for again?”

“Work.” I sighed as if it were the worst thing in the world. “Not even time off to join the party.” Not that I wanted to be anywhere near that mess.

“I’ll have a drink for you.” He gave me a nod and a smile as the plane came to a stop and the seatbelt light clicked off.

“Better yet, have a king cake.” The last thing the kid was going to need was more alcohol.

I stood up, grabbing my bag from the overhead compartment and waiting my turn until I could deboard the plane. From there, I followed the swarm of people on their way to retrieve their luggage. Martha’s cousin,

Ron, had promised to meet me at the airport, and while I normally wouldn't like to call in favors like that, I was glad to see him waiting by the luggage carousels with a sign saying *Martha's Boss*.

"You must be Ron." I held out my hand, and he gave it a shake. "Thanks for coming to get me. I just need to find my bag and we can be off."

That finding the luggage part turned out to be easier said than done, and, an hour later, we were on our way to the hotel.

"Given the traffic, it's probably going to be a good forty-five minutes to get there." He apologized as his GPS redirected him to avoid an accident. "It can be like this."

"How long have you lived here?" I asked, not hearing the accent that I was anticipating.

"I came here to go to school and then kind of stayed." He went on to explain all about his years at school, meeting his now spouse, and moving up the ladder at his current job—the forty-five minutes flew.

"My cousin told you, you are getting one of the shit rooms, right?" He pulled into a little spot with a sign labeled *Reserved.* "I'd gladly give you one of the upgraded ones, but this weekend is the busiest of the year, and it is all I have."

"I don't mind. This was a very last minute trip." *And the old room is the one I need.* "Is the entire hotel upgraded except mine?"

"No, there are a few. They should have done them all in order and banged them out, if you ask me. The higher ups didn't want to move people, so they went in as people left their rooms, and, with a few of those, that meant months and months."

I couldn't picture a job requiring that kind of stay away from home even though I'd heard it had become more and more common over the past few years.

"It sounds like a mess." I waited for him to reach for his door handle just in case his babbling offered an opportunity for me to ask him about the man I was looking for.

"It is." He reached for the handle.

Oh well, it was worth a shot.

The front lobby was bustling with people all just congregating. My best guess was they were meeting for dinner, possibly work related given their attire, and even though that didn't feel like the kind of situation the person I was looking for would be a part of, I scoured the group hoping for the best.

I didn't find him.

"Where are they from?" I slid my credit card and ID over the counter to Ron who had moved around back for me, his coworker giving him a weird look but not saying a thing.

"Some tour group or something?"

I sure had that wrong.

"Here is your key with the internet passcode and room number on it." He handed me a small cardboard folder the size of a credit card. "There is a pantry to your left if you want or need anything, the pool is around to the right, just follow the signs, and there is breakfast behind you from six to nine each morning. You're on the fourth floor and turn left. Your best bet is to take the elevator up, but if you hate yourself, the stairs are to the right of it."

"Thanks. And thank you for helping with all this."

"My cousin would never let me hear the end of it

if I didn't." He was right on that one. Martha was…well, Martha.

"I'll be sure to tell her how helpful you were."

I wheeled my little suitcase behind me, my carry on slung over my shoulder, and climbed into the elevator, pressed number four, and watched as the door closed. After I dropped my things off in my room, I'd make a game plan.

The elevator dinged, and I walked out then turned left, looking for 420. I arrived at my door, slid the key in. Nothing. Did it again. Nothing. I jiggled the doorknob just in case.

This time, the result wasn't *nothing*. The door swung open, and I found myself face to face with the man from my dreams.

"You." I gasped at the same time he leaned in close and said the same exact thing.

Chapter Six

"How did you find me?" He stepped out of the way.

I walked inside, unsure what else to do. "I didn't. Not really. My assistant found me the hotel, and I'm not sure how I ended up at your room."

He stood there, the door still open, and I reached past him to close it. If we were going to talk about anything real, it was best not to have anyone walking by listening in.

"Are you fourth floor?" he asked.

"Yeah."

"That's the problem. They started the numbering in the basement, so the fourth floor is really the third, but the elevator company… They need to fix it. I've had drunks here almost every night since I checked in."

I wasn't following his explanation, but I cared not at all how I'd ended up standing in front of him, only that I was.

"And when was that? The checking in, I mean?" I

dropped my carry-on bag onto the floor, my shoulder no longer able to hold the weight of it comfortably.

"A week ago yesterday."

I tried to count back and figure out how his showing up here meshed with my connecting with him and the little girl, but my brain was too aflutter with what to do next. I anticipated spending most of the weekend trying to find him, and now that I had without even trying, I wasn't sure what to say or do, especially since he knew who I was.

How did that even work?

"You know who I am," I stated, not really asking, but at the same time needing to hear the words.

"The woman who visits me." He sucked in a breath. "How do you do that, and why? At first, I thought you were Lucy's mother haunting me, but then I saw you at dinner, and you're not her."

"You saw that?" That was just a dream. He shouldn't have been there.

"I was, and for the last few seconds, I saw you so clearly. It's been a long time since I could do that." There was a sadness to the last part which compelled me to hug him. Except I didn't. He was a stranger, and none of this was making sense. Adding physical comfort to the mix would only confuse things even more.

"Why are you not freaked out by this?" Because a normal person would be. "It isn't everyday someone from your dreams walks into your awake days and announces, 'Here I am.' Shouldn't you think I'm crazy or something?" I asked to buy myself a few seconds so I could figure out the scene before me. Had I not possessed an extremely firm grasp of my gift, I'd have thought myself dreaming.

"First of all, I'm the one who has said the craziest things since you walked in." On that, he was right. "And second of all, I am part of a team that has seen a lot of things most people would dismiss or think crazy. So I guess I'm numb to that."

That caught my attention.

"Team?"

"I work for the Phoenix Agency." As if that meant anything to me. "We help people who can't be helped using traditional avenues."

"You mean like Lucy." And suddenly it felt like the cards were stacked more in our favor. If he had a team backing him, maybe paired with his research and my ability we might stand a chance of getting to her in time. So far, her captors had kept her fed and, from everything I'd seen, left her untouched—if they had wanted to kill her, they'd have done so already.

"Yes, like Lucy." He held his hand up, covering one of his eyes. "Why don't you sit over there…um, I'm sorry, I don't know your name."

I sat on the couch, my body sinking into the old cushion and loving the way it almost hugged me. "I'm Everly. Everly Jones. And I don't know your name either."

"Hal. Hal Sims." And now the sexy man of my dreams had a name. "Do you want a water or something? No offense, but you look pretty wrecked."

"No offense taken. I haven't slept in a while, but sometimes there are more important things than sleep." I yawned despite my best effort not to. "Like finding Lucy."

"And if you can't focus, what good are you?"

“How about you tell me who Lucy is, what happened to her, and we can go from there?”

“Or you can get a nap and be refreshed enough to help me figure out part two of your question.”

Stubborn man. Stubborn, stubborn man. How was I ever going to help the little girl if he was pushing me to nap of all things.

“You do know it is odd to meet someone and then have them tell you to take a nap. For all I know, you are a serial killer luring me here to wear my skin or something.” A yawn forced itself upon me by the end of my rebuttal. *Well done, Everly.*

First of all, you came to me. Second of all, this entire thing is odd, so picking out the tiniest little bit to highlight does nothing to prove your point.” He rubbed his left eye, his right one squinting. “And third of all, I didn’t say you needed to nap here. I just need you ready, and you clearly are not ready to think right now.” He reached in his pocket, pulled out his phone, and seconds ahead of him pressing the button, I figured out what he was doing.

“I don’t need you to”—*Snap!*—“take my picture.”

He held the phone out to me, and the person staring back looked like she was sixty years old after spending the night at a kegger, drinking everyone under the table.

Crap. He was right.

"Fine. I'm not saying you are right, but I'll nap. But then we work until we find her. Deal?"

He nodded. "And I will get everything together and order food while you nap. How does that sound?"

"Not like a serial killer," I conceded, and then, despite all my better judgement, I curled up on the couch and fell sound asleep.

Chapter Seven

Pizza. I ran to the door, the scent wafting through the room, beckoning. When was the last time I ate? And why was I smelling my dream? It wasn't a normal part of my gift and never part of my natural dreams.

"Thank you." Hal's voice sounded far away, yet not.

Because you are only half asleep, silly.

I forced myself awake, stretching my arms out and making contact with something hard. No, not something, someone. Crap, I hit the poor guy.

"Sorry," I mumbled as I cracked my eyelids open. "How long have I been asleep?"

The fogginess from ripping myself from REM sleep faded as he came into sight holding three pizza boxes with a paper bag that was stapled shut sitting on top.

"It was my fault. I shouldn't have been standing so close." He shrugged. "And you've been asleep for a few hours. You talk in your sleep, you know."

Of course, I did. Which was why I never should've entertained the notion of sleeping anywhere but in my hotel room. Alone.

So why did I sleep here? *You were just too tired to make good decisions.*

"Did I say anything interesting?" Or embarrassing?

"You pretty much just mumbled."

Oh, he was lying. But in a gentlemanly way, which was good since the first part of my stupid dream had me kissing him out of nowhere because that was what we had time for. A girl's life was in danger and *boom*, my libido decides to kick in for the first time in far too long.

"Thank you for being kind." Might as well let him off the hook.

"Dinner?" He stepped over to the table and set down the pile of food. "I didn't know what you liked, so I got a bunch of things. Pepperoni pizza in case you were traditional about such things, a gluten-free version just in case the crust was an issue, a huge salad with the chicken on the side in case you are vegan, and a burger medium well. That I knew you liked because…you know."

I did know, too. That dream was the oddest out of all of them so far. Who dreams about a date where you get food and black holes as gifts? Me. That was who.

"I'll just wash up a quick second." I stood up, stretching again, and went to the bathroom to splash some water on my face and wash the grime of travel from my hands. By the time I returned, the food was spread across the counter buffet style.

"You didn't need to do all of this." I picked up a plate. "But thank you. Which is gluten free?" He pointed to the one pizza, and I passed it by, grabbing a huge slice of pepperoni pizza. "Thanks. I need this crust like my next breath," I teased, portioning up a bit of salad and half the burger to go with it.

He grabbed a couple of slices and the rest of the burger, not pretending the greens were going to pass his lips, and sat down across from me.

"I tried to organize everything, but really it feels so random, which is why they called me in the first place. I tend to be the guy who can find the unfindable, or at least I was until this case." He grabbed his pizza and bit off a huge piece.

"Who hired you? Her parents?" I started with my burger as he put down his pizza.

"You don't know," he said softly. "Maybe we should start with what you do know and I can fill in the blanks."

"I know her name is Lucy, but you told me that in a dream. Other than that, I mostly just know that she is scared and cries a lot. I tried to comfort her." And failed most of the time, but it was the least I could do until I was able to get something concrete. *Please let connecting with Hal on this plane be what I was supposed to do.*

"Nothing else?"

"Just a memory from a year or two ago. There was a weird guy there asking her questions, and then she screamed for her mom." I thought back to that dream. Lucy had been trying to tell me something…something important. "He seemed to know about her gift or at least suspect."

"Her gift?"

"I think she is like me…only a lot stronger, or will be once she has some training. She called me to her, and I am thinking she is the reason I came to you, unless you have a gift, too. Do you?"

"I didn't think so until that dream with us. And now…now, I'm not sure."

Well, didn't that just change things?

"Let's get back to that, then." I got up and grabbed a notebook from my bag, "Here is everything I remember, including a really horrible sketch of the man in that one dream. He was pretty hidden, so I'm not sure a snapshot could even help much." I handed him the notebook, glad I decided to create it.

As a rule, I felt dreams were too private to record. Lucy's case was different. She needed me to make sense of them all, to be able to solve the mystery of her location, to save her. I could burn them later, but for now, the information the notes contained could be a matter of life and death.

He took out his phone. At first, I thought he was trying to take photos, but then his real intent came into view…he was using the camera as a magnifying lens.

“You have your dreams with me in here, too.” He looked at me over the top of the page.

“I don’t want to miss anything.” I shrugged, not wanting him to be embarrassed. Not that there was anything embarrassing in them.

“You were afraid you would forget I’m a ‘hottie?’” He smirked, the first smile I’d seen from him since entering his temporary home.

“I wrote what I wrote.” I grabbed my burger in an attempt not to die from embarrassment.

Chapter Eight

We finished eating in silence as he read through my notes, not commenting again, simply closing the book when he was done and eating his now tepid food.

I got up, cleaning up as much of the mess as I could as he ate. When he was finished, I cleaned up his mess as well. Then he rose and walked into the bedroom. The silence normally would have had me on edge, but for some reason it suddenly felt necessary, like he needed to process everything I'd flung at him or something.

About ten minutes later, he emerged and point to the couch that was adjacent to the kitchen table. "Shall we move to the living room?"

I let out a giggle at his dry humor, getting up and finding my spot on the couch again, this time much more able to focus than I had been earlier.

In his hand was the folder from the dream, and he placed it on the coffee table in front of me as he sat in the only other chair in the space.

"You saw it that night, right? All the things in here?" He bit his bottom lip as he squinted in my direction.

"Sort of." I didn't want to make things as awkward as I was about to out of necessity. "In the dream, I can only see as well as you do for some things…sort of like I am looking through your eyes even though I'm not. That probably doesn't make any sense." I let out a sigh. "So what I am saying is—"

"You need to look at them because my eyes are for shit?" he snapped, the softness of his voice not hiding the hurt.

"Something like that. I didn't mean it to be anything but… Never mind."

"No, I should be the one apologizing. It's still a sensitive subject with me. My condition is…let's just say it is fairly new." He tapped the folder. "You should read through this and see if anything clicks."

I took the folder, and he held up a finger.

"You know what? Maybe…"

"Maybe?" I asked unsure what he was getting at.

"Let me give you the abbreviated version first." I

put the folder back down. "We don't know how long Lucy has been gone. Her parents were found dead a couple of weeks ago, but their bodies were… It wasn't pretty, and the people who did it did a good job making them possible to identify while impossible to determine the time of death and did an even better job burying the entire thing. It was somehow deemed a suicide, and Lucy was mentioned nowhere in any of the paperwork, her bedroom completely empty, and the fresh paint in the office suggesting that had once been her room. I've never seen anything like it, and trust me…I've seen things."

"So, I'm right, and this isn't just a random child snatching." My stomach dropped. What kind of a sicko or sickos would do something like this?

"No. It's not. And if it weren't for something Lucy had written at school, we wouldn't have anything." He opened the folder and pulled out a piece of paper. "It was supposed to be a story about her spring vacation, the one to Disney World she had been telling everyone about, but… Well, read it."

And read it I did. It started out with her discussing

how she had dreamed about visiting the princesses forever and how sad it was that she would be gone before then. She said she wasn't scared or sad though because—

"You got to the part about you, I see."

I nodded then read and reread the words over and over again.

My new mom will find me wearing bright-purple and green beads and a mask. She will be my princess, the princess from my dreams.

"I don't understand… Why would the teacher even connect this, and how do you connect to this all?" My eyes stayed glued to the words. *The princess from my dreams.*

"Her teacher is my sister, or was until she was pulled out of school two months before the parents were found. She is how I discovered the case. She got the police report online, and the investigating officer said it was a different couple. But her gut told her that it wasn't. She said their departure from school was just too bizarre for that, and called me instead."

He pushed some papers to the side then handed me

one he unburied. "They withdrew her, citing they were moving to Montana. We found no evidence that was ever in the works…the Montana part."

I looked down at the paperwork from the school.

"And this is their signature?" I tapped where the scribbles sat.

He nodded. "Yeah, they did it in office. We checked on that."

"And why did your sister call you and not the police?"

"She called me to ask if she should call the police, and as she told me the details I talked to my boss, and here I am." There was a lot missing in the middle there, but there would be time for that after we found her. And we would find her, too, her story proved it. But how to make that happen was another thing altogether.

"What if she is the reason I…um, we had that dream? To show us what she could do, I mean."

He didn't respond, as if digesting my words and trying to make sense of them.

"I mean, what if that is our future…and she wanted me to know I would find her and to believe the story?"

"You mean I will—*we* will..." He stopped speaking, silence filling the air for most of a minute when he finally said, "Maybe that was why."

I knew where his mind was going. Mine had already gone there. Would we really be celebrating our time together? Sure, I was attracted to him—how could I not be? Anyone interested in men would have him ping their radar. But there wasn't time nor the emotional energy for that. Even if we lived in the same place.

Chapter Nine

We spent the rest of the evening and well into the night going over his evidence piece by piece, and sure enough, there wasn't much there that felt like anything to me. Except that she was adopted. And in order to investigate that further, we would have to wait until morning.

"I need to go to bed," I finally said as the clock caught my attention. "If I don't, I won't be able to see Lucy." I had already planned on trying to actively ask her questions now that it was clear she knew what she was doing or at least knew she had some powers. Her school paper was proof or at least proofish of that.

"You should stay here. I'll keep the couch," he immediately offered.

"My room is fine." And didn't hold the temptation that Hal was quickly becoming. "And you are far too tall for this couch."

"And what if you need to tell me something?"

"I can walk the distance." I stood up, stretching,

my body not enjoying all of the sitting the day had entailed.

"I would feel safer with you here. I don't know why. I can't explain it, but it feels like you are in danger." His confession shocked me. "That's why I wanted you to nap here. And before you ask, no I have no facts or anything to back it up. It's just why I am, or usually am, good at this job. I have a strong sixth sense. I used to blame it on just putting pieces together, but after going to work for The Phoenix Agency, now I'm not so sure."

I needed to ask him more about this agency, but not now. Time was running low if I was going to be able to connect with Lucy. And if his gut or sixth sense or whatever was telling him I was in danger, I had no reason not to be a little cautious.

"I will stay on one condition…"

"I don't eavesdrop?" He filled in the rest for me, and while that wasn't what I had in mind…

"Two conditions, then. Don't eavesdrop and I get the couch." I crossed my arms as if I meant business.

"Done, if it is the only way, but honestly, I would

feel better if you were in the bedroom without the door to your back." He truly was worried which, in turn, made me worried.

"So I should put you with your back to the door?" Scenes from movies where people with shotguns blowing holes in doors flashed through my ridiculous mind, but once the idea was there, it only took root. "Maybe I don't want you there either. If you get shot sleeping, who is going to save me?" I sassed, but there was truth in my words. This might be his everyday gig, but I was a corporate sweetheart, not a spy or person finder or whatever you called his position.

"Then we will share the bedroom. I can sleep on the floor." He snatched my suitcase and marched on in as if it were a done deal.

"I can sleep on the floor." I followed after him with my carry-on in my hand. "It's only fair given this is your room."

"Everly." He turned around quickly, my suitcase now on a little bench designed for it. "I have slept in places that would give you nightmares. Trust me, the floor is fine for me."

"If you are sleeping on the floor, so am I." I set my carry-on on top of my suitcase, brushing past him.

"You should sleep on the bed. You needed to stretch from traveling. There is no way sleeping on the floor will help that." And then he began to crack up—not a little giggle, a full on belly laugh.

"What's so funny?" I asked, and he kept laughing.

"It's not." He said between breaths as his laughter subsided. "Not really."

"Fine. Whatever. Where are we sleeping, on the bed or the floor? Time is marching on."

"You will only sleep on the bed if I do?"

"It is either that or hearing you get shot to bits on the couch. So yeah, that is the option I pick." Weren't we quite the pair?

"Fine. And I wasn't laughing at you. I was just realizing my sister was right,"

"How so?"

"She said one day I was going to meet a woman as stubborn as I was, and given all the stress of this case, it hit me funnier than it should have. I just wanted you to know it wasn't you I was laughing at." He opened the closet, grabbed the blanket from the top shelf, and along with it, some extra pillows.

"I didn't... Okay, maybe I did think you were laughing at me, so thank you for the apology even if it did mean you called me stubborn."

"And aren't you?" His voice lifted slightly.

"Not as stubborn as you." I stuck out my tongue, and he smiled. How much could he see? That was a question better left until morning, after I saw Lucy. But ask it I would.

Chapter Ten

I threw on my shorts and T-shirt that I bought for bed, and, after quickly brushed my teeth, climbed right in.

"If you are on the floor," I scolded, "I'll be pissed." Were my last words to him.

I closed my eyes and snuggled into the bed, trying hard not to think of the man in the room and all the things I didn't know about him and was yearning to learn while, at the same time, feeling more comfortable with him than I even felt with Martha who was pretty much my closest friend. It had to be the dream walking connecting us. There was no other explanation I could come to.

After hearing the shower go on and then off, I figured out how much time I was spending on the near stranger and not sleeping. So, I did what I did every night as I headed off to slumber.

I breathed in.

One. Two. Three. Four. Five.

I held my breath.

One. Two. Three. Four. Five.

I exhaled.

One. Two. Three. Four. Five.

Repeat.

Repeat.

Repeat.

Repeat.

Repeat.

I woke, or dream woke as it were, in the same backyard as the last dream, only this time Lucy wasn't the Lucy of happy-turned-weird day past. No, this was the Lucy I first met, the one in confinement.

"You came." She took two steps closer. "I was worried."

"I stayed up too late," I said by way of apology. "But I knew I had to come. What is different today?"

"I hid the pills," she said softly. "When they find them, they will be mad. I'm scared about when they find them, but I needed to talk to you. Did you find him yet?"

"Hal?"

"The man who sees without seeing. I don't know his name." She spoke like someone far older than her years.

"Yes. I found him. Help me find you."

She looked up at me, and my breath hitched. Her eyes were closed, but only mostly, and the closer I got to her the clearer what I was seeing became. It was all I could do not to lose my dinner. Someone had sewn her eyelids shut, or mostly shut.

"It doesn't hurt," she reassured me as I gathered her in my arms. "They called it Taro-happy or something. The doctor promised them it was temporary but would solve their problem."

"What is their problem?"

"That I can communicate with people, and if I see things, so can they." She felt suddenly lighter, and I knew our time was drawing to an end. I let her go, stepping back only far enough to see her.

"They know you can do this?"

She nodded.

"How?" Did she not have someone like Grams teaching her from a young age not to? Of course, she didn't. She was adopted. They probably thought her *creative* or possibly *mentally ill*—something people with my skill had been called over the decade. At least the label "witch" followed by execution were no longer in the pocket of acceptable.

"They trained me to be this." Her voice faded with every word.

"Where are you, Lucy?" I asked as she was not much more than a projection.

"I don't know, but I am down not up. Down." And with that, she vanished.

I tried to force myself awake, needing to share all I'd discovered with Hal, but in this realm, his pull was already yanking me from the grass and back to the hotel room. Except this time, it wasn't his room I wound up in.

This room was darker. So much darker. I was unable to move, and it felt as if I had weights piled on me.

"I'm here." A small voice echoed in the small space I was confined to. No, not just a voice, Hal's voice only weaker. So much weaker.

"We are here, soldier. Please let us know where you are."

"I'm here," he spoke again only much softer.

I couldn't see him, and my body couldn't move to find him.

This had to be the past. He was no soldier nor would he be, not with his eyesight. His eyesight. He was showing me what happened, or part of it anyway.

"I found him, sir," another man shouted, and from there, everything went in warp speed, from clanging to I didn't even know what, but suddenly, there was a glimmer of light and then a ray and then the light was overbearing. We had been set free.

"Sims. Sims." Yet another voice called. "Can you hear me? I am going to help get you out of here. We heard the explosion and came as quickly as we could."

And from there, the scene changed again. I was sitting in a chair in a hospital room only not. The walls were makeshift or at least not permanent, and, on the bed, connected to all kinds of tubes and wires, his eyes completely bandaged and his arm in a cast, was Hal.

Beep.

Beep.

Beep.

Beep.

The sound of his heart monitor relieved me, comforted me in a way. Cognitively, I knew this was the past, but seeing it play out like this had it feeling very much like the present.

A man in a white coat came in, a clipboard in his hand, and his eyes filled with something I couldn't quite place…something not good.

"Hal Sims, I'm Dr. Livingston."

"Am I…am I going to make it?" The raspiness of his voice was one I recognized from watching my grandmother get sick and pass. He'd been on a respirator and not for a short period of time.

"Not going to sugar coat it for you, had someone asked me that two weeks ago, I'd have said I didn't know. You are a miracle."

"But."

"But you won't be the same. Your eyes… You may never regain sight."

Hal's silence at the doctors words hurt more than

if he had wailed.

And the scene shifted again, but not. I was in the same room, but it was later…or so the beard on Dr. Livingston would indicate.

"After we get the bandages completely off, please wait until we dim the lights way down to crack them open." The doctor and assistant removed the bandages, and there were so many. A lot of the layers were blood encrusted. My own eyes teared up at the sight of his injury, the last bit coming off and the doctor giving Hal a squeeze on the shoulder as he directed a nurse I had not even noticed to dim the lights. Then he gave Hal permission to open his eyes.

He saw nothing.

They raised the lights, and he still saw nothing.

A half hour and a lot of light rising later, he finally saw something. Something fuzzy and opaque. He was pointing in my direction. What the heck was that?

I didn't get to find out for the scene shifted once again.

This time, we are in an office, and he was wearing jeans and a slightly too tight T-shirt, and the doctor sitting across from him is not the same. On his left side was a woman I immediately recognized as his kin, their noses and chin so identical it was almost scary.

"And the cane can help you avoid collisions with things like chairs or the road when you don't see an upcoming curb."

"I don't need it. I can see enough." Hal's anger had the doctor flinching. Did he not see the anger was directed at himself, not the man there to help him? Hal blamed himself for this, as if he'd caused the explosion, and from what little I knew, that was very much not the case.

"You can, Hal. And maybe you always will, but having this in your toolkit in case you need it is prudent."

"Good day, Doctor." He stood up and walked out of the room, leaving the cane behind him and bumping into two different chairs along the way.

The rest of the room faded away as he left, and I ended up back in the green patch of grass, Lucy still not present. Softly at first then increasing with every breath, laughter echoed through the space. And not happy laughter, like the kind you hear at a comedy show or from kids witnessing a magic shoe. No, this laughter was reserved for horror movies.

I wanted to plug my ears. Instead, I forced myself to listen, hoping for a hint or a tiny morsel of a hint of who that was and where they were. I tried and tried until I could bear it no more, and I woke up screaming.

Chapter Eleven

"I got you. I got you," a voice so very far away said, but not one from my dream, not the evil one cackling. "I got you." The voice was closer this time, and I felt motion like I was in a boat only there was no boat. I was in New Orleans and in a bed. The world I woke up to becoming clearer by the second.

"I got you," he said again. *Hal* said again, and the motion was me rocking back and forth, but not alone… I wasn't alone. He'd enveloped me in his arms and was allowing me full range of motion while keeping me from being alone.

"I got you," he murmured again, this time close to my ear.

"You got me," I mimicked back to him as my body slowed, my face wet, my head pounding, my eyes still shut.

"Tell me what you need."

"This. Just let me come out of this not alone." I'd never had an experience like this one, although my grams told me that when I first started to show signs of my gift, I would wake up with a scream. But it'd always been the fear of realizing what was happening and not what I'd seen or heard. This was different. So, *so* very different. Like I was being toyed with.

Like I was prey.

We sat like that, me in his protective arms, as my heart slowed to normal and I put the pieces together of what I had seen, both of us silent until the slam of a neighbor's door and loud giggles erupted from the next room.

"I guess pensive time is over," I tried to tease as I opened my eyes to find the room dark, but not quite black, the light from the smoke detector blinking in the corner.

"Are you alright?" he asked tentatively.

"No…yes…maybe." I hugged him back. "Thank you."

"I felt so helpless. Can you tell me what happened, or is that under the *eavesdropping* clause?" He pulled away, most likely to give me some space, and I instantly wanted to be back in his arms.

"It started out with me seeing Lucy, only this time she could talk to me and…this isn't random. I mean, I knew it wasn't, but now I *know* it is not. They sewed her eyes shut, well mostly shut. They don't want her to be able to give anyone clues about where she is, so they took her eyes from her." The animals. Who did that? And to a kid?

"They performed a tarsorrhaphy on her to keep her blind?" His voice hitched.

"It has a name? People do this to others?" My stomach lurched.

"It is a medical procedure—at least in most cases. I didn't show you this part, but they did one on me while I was healing. It gave me the best chance of seeing again, not to prevent sight. That's—"

"Barbaric." I took his hand in mine. "Thank you for showing me what happened to you." It wasn't the right time to tell him, but I felt compelled to let him know how much it meant, especially after he was here for me so perfectly when I was torn from my sleep.

"You wanted to know, but you didn't ask." He half shrugged. "I didn't show you the blast because I don't have anything to show. It was a normal mission, and then I woke up to people helping me out of the rubble."

"You are so strong."

"Says the woman who flew to find a stranger to save another stranger she met in a dream." He squeezed my hand. "Speaking of dreams, was the tarsorrhaphy why were you screaming? It felt more like fear than horror."

"Felt?"

"I was sleeping when fear overtook me, and somehow, I recognized it as yours. I woke up to you covering your ears, and then your scream came." He explained as if it were the most normal thing ever. It wasn't.

"After I saw you, I ended up back where I'd last seen Lucy, in the grass where I witnessed her past. Only this time, she wasn't there. Someone else was. I couldn't see them, but I could hear them."

"What did they say?"

"That's the thing…they didn't *say* anything. They only laughed. Cackled really. Their voice increased in volume by the second."

"You're quaking." He held his arms open. Closing the small distance between us, I curled up in them.

"I think he is hunting." I spoke the words that I had been mulling in my head, the truth of them ringing far too clearly for my liking.

"For children?"

"For people like me…people who can dream walk. And he is using Lucy as bait."

"We will get them and save her," he vowed. "And I will keep you safe."

"Can you maybe…I need to sleep."

He let me go immediately, moving to the side to give me space, the exact opposite of what I was wanting—needing.

"No, I mean, maybe if you don't mind, can you hold me while I sleep. I think maybe if you do, I can anchor myself to you and not end up *there* again." It was only a theory, and if it had been anybody other than Hal, I'd have called it a crackpot theory at that. With Hal though, there was a connection. Maybe it was a latent gift he had, or possibly it had something to do with the explosion making him more amenable to altered dream states, or maybe it was just him and the connection I felt to him even before we met. Whatever the case, something was there, and it was worth a try. I couldn't go back to that evil laughter again, not until I had some decent rest to fortify me.

"Lay down." He patted my pillow, and I did as he'd said. He lay beside me. "Do you want my arm as your pillow?"

It took me a half second longer than it should have to figure out what he was saying, and I picked my head up in response, setting it back down on his arm as soon as he was settled, and then scooched back to be his little spoon, something I'd never allowed myself to do with anyone one out of fear of falling asleep and inadvertently giving away my secret.

It felt nice—safe—comforting, and I found myself dozing off without having to do any breathing exercises or counting, just feeling secure in his arms.

A girl could get used to this.

Chapter Twelve

"Morning," his deep voice, still heavy with sleep, greeted me as I opened my eyes, the sunlight already cracking through the curtains. "How did you sleep?"

"Like a normal person." Or at least how I imagined normal people slept. I remembered nothing other than the feel of his arms around me until I woke up. Not a dream. Not a walk. Nothing. It was fan-freaking-tastic. "Be careful, I may take you home with me."

I stretched out my toes, feeling better than I had in far too long.

"I'd not have a problem with that…unless you have a cathole."

I rolled onto my side so I could get a better look at him. He was on his back, except the warm arm that was still under me. How the thing didn't fall off by now…? His lazy smile accentuated his dimple on the left cheek, and his whiskers were just peeking through.

"Define cathole?"

"A cat who is equal part feline and asshole—a cathole. My sister has one…he pooped in my shoes twice last time I visited. Now those suckers stay on my feet or in a cabinet. Done. Cathole."

"I have a cat, but I wouldn't call him a cathole. Maybe a caty-ass…no, that doesn't work."

He chortled all sleepy and sexy. "And what was caty-ass supposed to be blending?"

"Lazy ass—very much did not work, but yeah, Calvin is a nice cat. You'd like him. He doesn't poop in shoes." And if sister's feline was his barometer, he needed to meet some more cats.

"I should get up and make a plan for the day." He wiggled his arm slightly, and I picked my head up so he could extract himself.

"I have one…maybe…I was wondering how much technology does that agency have at their disposal?" My fingers itched to rub his cheek, to see how his whiskers felt against my skin. Instead, I folded them under my cheek.

"Not too shabby. Why. What do you have in mind?"

“How concerned would they be with breaking protocol and possibly a few laws?” I pushed myself up to sit.

“I’d imagine not too concerned at all. My guy loves a challenge.” He sat up, the blanket falling from him to reveal his shirtlessness—his muscular shirtlessness—the muscular shirtlessness I would not trace with my fingers or my tongue.

“Let’s break into some adoption records.”

“You know how to have a good time.” He winked and stood. “I’ll call my guy and set things up, and you can have the bathroom first.”

“I’ll hurry.”

“Don’t. Charlie is a talker. Chances are he will still be asking me questions when you get out of the shower.”

And sure enough he was.

“No. This is great. Thanks Charlie.” He finished scribbling something onto his notepad and looked up at me with a smile. “Charlie found the agency she was adopted from. They are not, shall we say, legal which is great news.”

In what world were illegal adoptions good news?

"Charlie is getting us an appointment today as a well-to-do couple that was turned down for adoption and whose bio clock is screaming at them." He smirked. The man was loving whatever plan he and his friend had concocted far too much.

"And then what? I distract them and you put a magical stick drive into a secret computer and we get all their data?" I was only half kidding. I mean, people did that on television, right? That or digging through file cabinets which people didn't even really use anymore.

"I was thinking more about flashing a badge and making a threat until they shared information, but sure…let's get all spy guys on them."

My jaw dropped. Threats? What did we have to threaten them with? We couldn't be the only one who knew there was some shady shit going down there.

"Kidding." He handed me the notebook. "We go in and interview them blah blah blah…try to get to the next step of things, and we use Lucy's parents as the people who told us about them all those years ago…"

I glanced at the notebook which contained an address and not much else.

"So we basically get them to say things they think we already know."

"Exactly. Now no offense, but we are going to need to go shopping. So I better get my shower on."

"Shopping?"

"Shopping. I don't know about you, but nothing I have here looks like anything a well-to-do father-to-be would wear." He padded off to the bathroom. "Charlie should have our appointment time soon."

"I'll go put some rich girl clothing on, then." I was only half teasing.

"If you have well-to-do want-to-be-mama attire, feel free to put it on. But if not, don't worry, I have my black card." He winked and walked the rest of the way to his destination.

I pulled out my iPad and began to search all about adoption, trying to prepare myself for any questions they might have. The big ones, we would need to discuss in the car. Where we lived, what we did for jobs, would we use fake names…all of that.

Unexpectedly, I came across a lot of anti-adoption blogs. I hadn't known there was such a movement and wondered why people didn't want these children to have families, and then I opened up the first, then the second, then the third blog, and all of them had a common theme: Babies were being sold or extorted from a family and then sold. It was a huge business.

"What is wrong?" Hal stood behind me. I had been so absorbed in the article I'd been reading I hadn't even heard the bathroom door open.

"I was researching what to expect at our meeting and fell down a rabbit hole."

"A dark one?"

"So very. There are people who actively work towards getting women to give up their babies, sometimes with threats. I had no idea." And I would've understood if this had been just one rambling person on the internet, but what I found was a lot of rambling persons telling similar stories. Could it really be a thing? My stomach lurched at the notion.

"It gets uglier than that." He squeezed my shoulder. "And because the big money comes from the wealthy, somehow, it is often able to get in under the radar. Dimes to dollars the article you were just reading will be down within the day. They are really good at covering tracks. They have had to adjust since it became more challenging for people to adopt from foreign countries."

"How do people not stop this?"

"Because money buys you a lot of invisibility." He held out his hand for me. "Shall we go? I'd like to be ready in case Charlie gets us in early."

I would like to get us in with arrest warrants.

How could people be so awful?

Chapter Thirteen

"This feels weird." I played with the rings on my finger. Hal had been right, looking the part included wedding and engagement rings, but still…

"Because I'm not your husband?" he whispered.

Oddly enough, that was not at all why. It was such an in-your-face, get in the way, he must've cheated on me to buy me something this big kind of ring.

"Because it is ginormous and gaudy."

"Which is the way it would be, I think." He handed the jeweler his black card, and even with them being good fakes, they cost more than I felt comfortable with him spending. But he insisted. "Now for you…you wouldn't want something like this, real or otherwise. I see you doing a diamond alternative to avoid unethically sourced diamonds, and something low profile, perhaps with an inscription so the good parts were only for you to see."

For a man who had vision issues, he saw me better than anyone I'd ever dated, and we were only pretending to have a relationship.

“Tanzanite, embedded so it isn’t catching on everything.” I tapped his ring, “And you would be all about those silicone rings, I’m thinking.”

The man came back with a slip for him to sign and wished us well.

“Lunch, Mrs. Simmons?” He held out his arm, his *undercover* name still amusing me as much as when he first came up with him. Who took a fake name almost identical to their own? Hal. That was who.

“Lunch.” I took his arm, and we walked out of the mall jewelry store, stopping long enough to see which direction the food court was in. Thankfully, the place was good and dead and we were able to grab some food and find a table off to the side.

“Not the fanciest meal, but there is something about food court yums.” I took a forkful of my Chinese.

“So, will this be our first date…if they ask? You eating Chinese and me a gyro in a mall food court?”

I liked the sound of that—of this being a date. Forget that this was the worst timing in history, that

100 percent of our time needed to be spent on finding Lucy, and that if we did the long distance thing, everything would flop, not to mention that he never once expressed any interest. Yeah, leave all that out, and I liked the sound of it a lot.

Maybe it was that stupid dream getting into my psyche. As if I had the ability to see the future as nice as that one was and as real as that one was.

"Sure." I ran through our story from start to finish in my head. We were set up by a mutual friend who became our best man—his name was Charlie—and we instantly fell in love. After years of trying, we discovered that my body was incapable of carrying a child. If they asked for more details, we'd just say it was too painful to talk about and hope they dropped it. We were married in Hawaii on the beach, a destination wedding in June. He worked in finance, and I used to be in marketing but was now a housewife. We had a cat named Cat.

We only hoped that was enough for us to improvise our cover.

"Excellent. Can you give me a spoiler, then?" He

bit into his gyro, and I nodded.

"Oh you mean like make one up," I said after the silence lasted too long. "It ended with froyo?"

"I was hoping for it ending with a kiss, but froyo works if I can have chocolate chips and gummy bears on mine." He winked at me.

"Don't the gummy bears get hard?" His phone buzzed, and he answered it, which meant it had to be Charlie.

"Hey. What's the good news." Pause. "Excellent." Pause "You are a miracle worker." Pause. "Yeah, send it all my way." Pause. "For serious. I'll update you as soon as I can." He slipped his phone back into his pocket then looked at me. "I am going to need to get you a better meal after our meeting, because it is go time." He stood up, gathering my tray and his. "I promise it will be a good dinner."

If only he could promise it would be a good meeting.

I drove us the half hour to the agency which, based on the information Charlie had sent us, was far more baby selling business than agency, specializing in "discreet and expedited" adoptions for only the finest future parents which, upon further reading, meant rich, not decent since they didn't even pretend to do a home visit or any of the normal things one would expect. The documents proved them to be the polar opposite of the "compassionate agency that brought new hope to children longing for forever home."

By the time we arrived, I was good and ready to go in and shut the place down singlehanded, the only things stopping me? The vision of Lucy sobbing with her eyes sewn closed, and the warm hand embracing mine.

Chapter Fourteen

"Your attorney suggested that you were having difficulty with standard adoptions. Care to elaborate on that?" the pointy nosed man asked out of nowhere.

Upon entering, we were greeted at the door by a grandmotherly older woman who whisked us into a private office, citing that they liked to ensure everyone's privacy, which made sense seeing as we weren't in the reception area for even a full minute. Then another woman of similar age came in and asked us all the questions we were expecting about how we met and if we were still in love and blah blah blah.

I'd thought that was the interview but no. It was another gatekeeper. Then we were moved to the office we were currently in with our *adoption counselor*, who, so far, had only asked financial questions to make sure they matched with the paperwork Charlie sent over on our behalf—which they by some miracle had matched. Then we went straight to the *why did someone else think you were unfit* line of questioning.

"You see…" I began, not sure where I was going and crossing my fingers something would come to me. Hal's hand gave my knee a gentle squeeze, the one we had decided in advance would mean he had this question handled.

His hand had been squeezing me a lot since we'd arrived in this office. At least, I felt like I held my own in the first one.

"Because…I'm going blind. I was visually impaired last year. I'm legally blind now, and in another year, I will be almost completely blind." Damn. There was truth in his voice, and my eyes teared up. To some extent, I knew his eyes weren't good, but being completely blind…that had surprised me.

"Genetic?" the man asked coldly.

"No. Head injury. At first, it was just the one, but the second one has been playing catch up."

I placed my hand on the top of his.

"Many blind people are amazing parents," I piped in.

"Indeed, but it does mean that things might cost a

little more—you know, to get the gears greased." He scribbled on a paper and slid it in Hal's direction, changing his mind midway and sliding it to me instead. I picked it up, looked at it, forced myself not to gasp at the insanely large figure, and handed it to Hal who took out his phone.

"You can't take a picture," the man snatched the paper from his hand. "You know the rules." We didn't, not really, but if we had, did he not think we might be sneaky enough not to whip out the phone like that?

"He uses it as a magnifying lens." I censured him and snatched it right back because fuck that.

Using his phone, Hal looked at the number, and from the expression on his face, was trying his best not to smile at my bitch slapping the man.

"We can accommodate this." He slipped his phone back into his pocket and out of sight. "Riddle me this, sir, how are we to know we are getting a, shall we say, quality child?"

"There are no guarantees when it comes to children, sir. You love a child because it is yours." Which was the perfect thing to say. Except it wasn't. It sounded more like an offer on the table than their meaning at face value. I couldn't even figure out what he did to give me that impression, but there it was.

"Our friends, the ones who told us about you when they adopted almost eight—was it eight years ago that Nancy and Ray adopted dear sweet Lucy?" I turned my attention to Hal.

"About that, yes. I miss them. We should probably get back in touch." They had moved into his sister's school district when Lucy was halfway through kindergarten, giving us a prebuilt excuse for not seeing them anymore. *Well played, Hal. Well played.*

"You mean the Bowmans?"

Hal and I both responded in the affirmative.

"They…they…" He stopped his speaking, and for a fraction of a second, I saw that he knew they were gone. "They were a perfect fit for their little girl." He pivoted away from what I was sure had been his telling us of their demise. I could just feel it.

"Lucy was such a *gifted* child when she was young," Hal said, hinting at her true gifts. This place could simply be a baby factory, not that there was anything simple about that, but it could also be something so much more…so much darker. And mister pointy nose was our doorway in.

"I'm sure she still is. Probably more so. Gifts grow with age and training." I let that simmer for a half a second and then tacked on, "Last I talked to Nancy, they were settling in to an excellent school. Schools make an education."

"For some kinds of giftedness they do." Hal spoke softly as if only to me.

"Were you interested in…a possible…"

"A unique ability?" Hal bounced back, and the man's smile creeped up. "You have seen my financials," he reminded the man who was now practically beaming.

"There is never a guarantee you see, but we do have some special children from time to time. Anything you are particularly interested in?"

That was too easy. It was creepy how a lot of money and some name throwing could open doors—doors to evil, but doors nonetheless.

"Given my career, a little foresight never hurt

anyone," was all Hal had to say before a number was thrown at us, nondisclosure papers hurled our way, and three pictures—one of a toddler, another a newborn, and the third a pregnant mom—were all thrust at us.

"The cost will be a bit more for the baby waiting to be born, you have to understand. Both his parents are strong in their gifts and going home from the hospital with a baby is far more valuable than a child who has already bonded with their *tutors*.

I didn't even ask what he meant by tutor, very much positive it was going to make me puke if I found out. The entire thing had me sick to my stomach as it was. The only thing saving us was many years of drama in school and sitting through horrible meetings with a smile plastered on my face.

Only this morning, I'd have referred to these meetings as evil. Because now I knew what an evil meeting really was.

"And the parents… How are you sure?" Hal held the picture very close to his face, squinting, a forced smile on his face.

"They are on staff, of course."

Chapter Fifteen

"That was— How does a place like that exist?" I screamed as we waited at the light near our on-ramp. "Shouldn't someone have ratted them out long ago? He didn't even pretend to not be doing what he was doing."

"They exist because greed exists. Yes, someone should have ratted them our long ago, except the people who find them desire what they are selling and are terrified of what would happen if the place really was shut down. And he didn't pretend only because Charlie did an excellent job of getting us set up for the meeting. He is really magnificent at what he does."

The light turned green, and I took my foot off the brake. "Should you be calling him?" Especially since we'd written a check for a ton of money as a *good faith* offering.

"He heard the entire conversation and saw all the things we did."

"Your phone was a camera?" I should have

guessed, except I hadn't.

"Not exactly. My tie tack is."

Because of course it was. I was in a spy movie whether I liked it or not. "Can he stop the payment?"

"Better…he can trace where it goes and then shut that down and redirect all their money to children's charities."

"I took far too long in the shower if I missed all that planning." I left the *how can he do that* part of my curiosity silent.

"Nah, Charlie and I just work well together."

I turned on my turn signal for the on-ramp. Then Hal squeezed my knee again, this time not to tell me to stop speaking because he could handle it. But because he just wanted to.

And I liked it. I liked it far too much.

"How about we stay on this road and find someplace to eat? I owe you a good meal after thwarting your lunch."

"I'm not going to argue with a hot man offering me a good dinner." The sass came out far too easily for me to notice my faux pas until after it was too late.

"Hot?"

"You know you are." I sighed overtly. "Now let's find us dinner."

A mile down the road we came to a little restaurant touting good steaks.

"Best Steaks in Louisiana three years running." I pulled into the driveway, already deciding this was our place. "And what's a fifty dollar steak when you just wrote a check for fifty thousand dollars?" Which was hella more than good faith in my opinion, but there it was.

"Not turning down a steak, that's for sure." I parked. It was late for lunch and early for dinner, making it the perfect time for a quiet dinner.

We got out of the car and walked inside.

"Follow me," the maître d' told us, then led us around the corner to a familiar room.

"Hal?"

He took my hand. "I know, love. I know."

We had walked into our dream, only not the same day—this was a year earlier, and he'd called me love. I knew it was his way of telling me he remembered the dream and it wasn't my imagination that this was the same place. But deep inside, just hearing that word felt good. Almost too good, given I'd known him for less than a day.

We were seated at a table, offered wine, and told the specials. I heard the noise of someone talking, but none of the words, as I sat, still in awe that we were in the place of my dreams. My dream had told the future. Or maybe Hal's dream had. That part was a bit hazy.

"Has this happened to you any other time?" I asked as soon as we were left alone. It wouldn't stay this quiet for long—I'd caught a glimpse of the reservations list, and there were plenty, just not quite yet.

"No." He bit his bottom lip. "Ummm maybe, actually. Not like this though, and never with someone else."

I picked up my water, taking a cool sip, allowing him time to elaborate. He didn't.

"I'm going to need more than that."

"Sometimes, I see things a bit early—an alarm going off five minutes ahead or time or someone passing away the morning they pass, things like that. I always assumed it had more to do with my ability to piece things together than sight, if that makes sense."

"And now you are thinking it is possibly something more?"

"I kind of hope it is given that it means I'm back here with you."

And the stupid waiter picked that moment to show up.

Was he serious, or had he been teasing? Argh. Why did the waiter have such poor timing? And really, did it matter? If he was teasing, it wasn't out of cruelty. And if he was serious, I could deal with being someone's crush, someone sexy and smart and brave is never a thing I'd turn down. If only we were meeting under better circumstances. If only we lived near each other. If only this had been a proper date. If only there weren't so many stupid if onlys.

Chapter Sixteen

My phone started to buzz, and I ignored it. Until it kept buzzing.

We'd only been back at the hotel for five minutes, and I wanted to relish the warm feeling that our dinner out had created for the few minutes we had to spare. Charlie had sent some more information we were going to need to weed through, and I wanted to get to bed on the early side to see if I could find Lucy when maybe she wasn't being monitored, which that maniacal laughter indicated might not be that often.

"Sorry, I murmured as I looked down to see my phone filled with pictures still populating and the message: *Call me*

"Work," I explained as I walked toward the window, hoping for better reception so the photos would populate already. And then they did, and I found myself stumbling.

"Hal?" He was already at my side by the time the words crossed my lips. "Look." I went to hand him my phone and realized my faux pas. “I mean…fuck…it’s him.”

His arms came to my shoulder, steadying me.

“Who?” He grabbed my phone as it buzzed again. After a moment, he handed it back. “Here.”

It was Martha again, this time calling me. “Martha, are you safe?”

“Yeah. What? Yeah, I’m fine.” She sounded anything but. “Someone came looking for you today. I sent the security footage. He was creepy as fuck and wouldn’t tell me why he wanted you, just kept saying it was a business venture, so I directed him to the big bosses, and he was all…never mind and left.” She sucked in a breath. “And so I figured he was a headhunter…you get those, you know?”

I held out my phone so Hal could hear better, the volume turned all the way up.

“I do.” All. The. Stupid. Time. I wasn’t sure why people thought if you were in a nice cushy job making amazing money you would want to jump ship for a startup, but they did. “What has you so freaked out?”

There was no way for me to ask her what I really

wanted to ask her. *He looks an awful lot like a guy I saw in a dream that was really a memory of someone I have never met but need to find quick before harm comes to her. So, did you by chance, hear his laughter so I can be sure?*

"Kallie from reception just invited me to happy hour." Like she did every time they worked a Friday shift. "And then I said, 'Too bad Everly is away.' And do you know what she said? She said that was what the guy who was in earlier said."

"Please connect the dots for me, okay?" And please let her not be saying what I thought she was saying.

"She told him where you were, and he pushed for exact details, and she… It feels off. Should I call the cops on him? Or am I being paranoid because of our training last month?" Which had been all about the scare tactics and how everyone was out to kill us all and we needed to have four thousand plans in place, so yeah, under normal circumstances, I'd have assumed it was her paranoia. But given I'd just seen him in a dream, I was just as concerned. No scratch that, I was twice as concerned.

"It's fine. He's probably just a headhunter who has no social skills. Next time, just ask for a card." How I pulled that off without my voice quacking was a mystery I would never solve, but I did then ended the call with a very brief chat about my flight.

"Can do, boss. Sorry to bother you. Is my cousin treating you well? How is the room?"

"I like the room I'm in quite nice. Your cousin looks like you, you know. He has your ears." Which she hated citing they looked elvish and I thought were adorable for the same reason.

"You did not tell him that, did you?" She was giggling. Safe to say I diffused her concerns. Now if only I could diffuse mine.

"No, of course not."

Hal stood there, giving me a *What the hell is going on?* look. Not that I could blame him, given the change in tone of the conversation. "Listen. I have to pee. Have fun at happy hour."

We said our goodbyes, and I hung up.

"We have a problem." I walked over to the couch

and sat down.

"I gathered." He joined me on the comfy cushions.

"Did you gather that the man I saw in Lucy's past was in my office looking for me? Because that's what just happened." I picked my feet up and hugged my bent legs. "This isn't just about Lucy. I suspected as much, but how is this about me?"

"I got you," he repeated the words from the night before, and I instinctively climbed onto his lap and allowed him to hold me close.

He had me.

But for how long? If that man could find me many states away, how long did I have before he traced me here? And how had he managed to find me in the first place? Lucy and I hadn't shared a dream with much more than me watching her, except that one time, and even that was on her turf.

I was missing something, but what?

"I need to go to sleep." I stood up, hating to leave his embrace, but not able to ignore the reality that my time was running out.

Chapter Seventeen

"Lucy!" I called, the fog surrounding me making my visibility pretty much nil, and the sound, echoing from so many angles, left me not much to focus on as far as directions. Dreaming could be a bitch like that.

She was singing, softly singing the lullaby I'd hummed to her so many times. But unlike me, she knew the words.

Round and round we travel

Till we travel no more.

But in this sleep you can travel

Twice the amount and more.

How could I have forgotten the words? It wasn't a lullaby, but more about preparing me for what was to come.

"Lucy!" I called again, my hands out straight so as not to run into anything as I took baby steps.

She kept on singing the refrain over and over.

"Lucy, how do you know that song?" I more mumbled than called out, unsure what I should be doing. A sense of urgency to get to find her done overwhelmed me, and just like that, the fog dissipated and the singing stopped. I was now standing in a room, a pink fluffy little kids room, and on the bed sat Lucy, only younger. And the woman I recognized to be her mother sat on the edge of her bed, her posture somehow menacing even as her face was plastered with a smile.

"Who taught you that song?" she asked.

Lucy just stared at her.

"I asked you a question. You can either answer it or get a spanking." Her mother's voice became so similar to that laughter that I found myself shivering from just the tone.

"Grandpa said you can't hit me anymore." Lucy pulled her knees up to her chest.

"And he said you need to obey." Her mother stood up. "Where. Did. You. Hear. That. Song."

"You won't believe me." She buried her head in her hands.

My blood was boiling and my heart breaking as I witnessed a glimpse of her childhood. No child should ever have to go through what she'd been through, and I didn't even know the half of it.

The mother looked to the girl then paused for most of a minute, eventually sitting beside Lucy and wrapping her arm around her. "I will believe you," she said, her voice much softer, even if not the least bit of sincerity shined through.

"Tell Mama. It's such a pretty song."

"I dreamed it," she finally admitted. "A little girl was listening to her grandmother singing it in my dreams. I asked her name. Thought we could be friends, but then she disappeared."

"We need to tell your grandfather about this." Her mother stood, all pretenses of kindness gone. "Get your shoes on. He will be well pleased."

And the fog was back and, with it, the singing.

"Who is your grandfather?" I crossed my fingers she would give me another glimpse. Instead, all I heard was her ear piercing scream followed by blackness and silence.

I sat down, not wanting to wander away, knowing I might not have a choice. I wanted to be where she was looking if and when she came back. I sat like this for what felt like hours but, in the dream realm, could easily have been seconds. Then I felt someone sit next to me, a small hand reaching for my own.

"I have but a minute. They think my dreams are over for the night, but they will soon see I am not asleep, and then they will know."

"Help me find you, Lucy."

"They always want me to help them find others. They want to find you. Don't let them find you."

"They? Who is they?" I could feel her skin begin to fade beneath mine.

"Grandpa and his kids."

"Your aunts or uncles?"

"No, people like me but adults. One called him gene. Does that help?" She was almost completely gone.

"So much. I will find you," I vowed.

"Just don't let them find you."

And then I was awake, as if pushed out of the dream realm altogether, and back into the here and now.

She was one powerful little girl.

I sat up, the room still dark, the bed beside me empty, and a glow coming from the next room. I climbed out of bed and padded over to find Hal bent over his computer at the table.

"What time is it?" I asked, and he snapped his head around. "Sorry, I didn't mean to frighten you."

"It's fine. I should have heard you get out of bed. Why are you up? It's only four." He stood, stretching.

"That should be my question." I walked over to the computer which was filled with very large print spreadsheets side by side. "What am I looking at?"

He reached around and pointed to the one on the left. "This is the money brought in by the adoption agency, and this"—he pointed to the second one—"is where the money ended up."

"Can you whole-picture it for me? It's too early to brain." I leaned back into him as naturally as if I did it every day. There was just something about Hal.

"Most of it is typical on this page—the electric company, the employees, taxes, that kind of thing." He took tapped the screen and pushed the spread sheet up.

"And then there is this…large deposits to a company that doesn't exist anywhere but on paper."

"What do you mean?"

"Charlie followed the money—he always follows the money." He half chuckled as if it were an inside joke. "And it all leads to this shell company, and that shell company leads to another." He let out a sigh.

"So we don't know who is getting the money?"

"We do know where it eventually leads. A medical research company. It's the in-between people, and there are a few from the looks of it, that we don't know. Charlie is working on it."

"Is that normal? To have so many misdirections?" I stared at the numbers…the numbers that made my head spin.

"Not usually, although sometimes." He retracted his arm. "Tea or coffee?"

"Tea and I'll make it. I'm the one who got some sleep." I walked to the small kitchenette and looked at the pathetic offerings of tea they had placed there as a courtesy. "Your choice is green or chamomile."

"Green, please."

I filled the kettle and placed it on the stove.

"Did you?" he asked.

"Did I what?"

"Did you really sleep?"

We'd had discussions on how some sleep didn't function as sleep for me, and the concern in question gave me a warm fuzzy feeling.

"Not really. But I found somethings out." I then proceeded to tell him my theory that Lucy had done more than dream traveling the way I did, that she potentially had seen my past in her dreams long before I knew of her existence, how horrible her mother had been, and finally about "grandpa" aka Gene.

The whistle rang, and I bounded into the kitchen to avoid disturbing the neighbors, not that they had given us a similar courtesy.

"Did she show you Grandpa?"

"She did not, but she told me not to let him find me. This feels so much bigger than a kidnapping."

"It has to be, or her murdered parents and her disappearance would've hit the news. If it weren't for my sister sensing something was really wrong, this would've all been swept under the carpet."

How often did that happen? It sickened me how much money could buy.

A buzzing sound filled the air. "Your phone?"

"Yes, but not one I should be getting called on." He rushed to his computer bag, bumping into the counter along the way, and fished out a flip phone, connecting it to a pair of headphones and flipping it over.

"What's up?" he almost snapped. "Say that name again?" Pause. "Fuck me." Pause. "And where can I find him? Yes, set up the team and we will get this done." He closed the phone.

"Do I want to know…I mean, can you tell me?"

"Yes and no." Let's get out of here. A man's gotta eat." He leaned over and grabbed a pen and paper scribbling on it. "I want you all to myself, so let's be the first in line for some beignets." He handed me the paper.

Bring cash only, not anything with a strip, chip, or battery.

I nodded.

"I could eat," I lied then rushed to get ready, leaving the place with only the clothing I was wearing and a wad of cash, Hal by my side. I wasn't sure what was happening, but I trusted him, and that was good enough for me.

Chapter Eighteen

We chatted on our way out, saying nothing at all, not really. There was so much I wanted to ask him, so much I wanted to know. Given how we got where we were, asking him felt dangerous, so I talked about everything but.

"My assistant says I should invest in better walking shoes," I said as we rounded the corner about a half mile from the hotel.

"Your feet hurt?" He stopped walking, and I came up alongside him. "I can slow down."

"You are too sweet. No, I was just randomly speaking because I—"

"Because that was the thing we were doing?"

"Something like that."

His hand brushed mine, and I grabbed it, wanting to feel his warmth. I leaned in close, grazing past his cheek so that anyone seeing us would assume a kiss was coming.

"I'm pretty freaked out right now," I confessed."

"I've got you."

"I know." I pushed back enough to see his face under the street light. "There are a lot of people who are going to hate themselves in the morning," I noted as a group of drunks giggled their way out of a bar we were passing.

"'Tis the way of Mardis Gras."

"I believe I was offered food." I pointed to a little hole-in-the-wall place that had a sandwich board out front promising the best breakfast in the city.

"Works for me."

We wandered into the cafe and were greeted with, "We have no liquor." Which was so telling of the day they'd had or were just starting.

"But do you have eggs?" I replied, and the woman just grunted, grabbed two menus, and indicated we should follow her.

It was remarkably quiet, given the number of people still wandering the streets.

"Good choice." Hal opened and closed his menu quicker than he could possibly have read it.

"Already decided?"

“They have french toast eggs benedict. What more is there to look at?” He had a point. It sounded yum.

“Agreed.”

The waitress came over and took our order, pouring coffee without us asking as if there was no way someone would walk in and not have coffee. Worked for me.

“Can we talk yet?” I didn’t want to push, but my anxiety was growing by the minute.

“Yeah. I just had to be sure we didn’t have anything that could be listening to us. I’ve been careless, assuming this was all about her. I apologize.”

“Your words need more…words.” I had little clue what he was talking about, except possibly our devices listening to us because, wasn’t that the way of things now?” “You have nothing to apologize for.”

“I kind of do. I should’ve seen it earlier. They wanted Lucy, true, but not for the reasons I had assumed.”

“They didn’t want her for her abilities?”

He got up then slid in next to me on my side of the booth, resting his head on my shoulder. I wrapped my arm around him, not hating the closeness.

"They had her for her abilities," he and whispered so only I could here. "They raised her to grow them. Something happened with her parents, the money train is sketchy—Charlie's words, not mine—but it appears they were hired to raise and train her…train her to find and recruit an army. An army whose weapon is dream walking. They are using her to get people like you."

"Get up. This is not that kind of place," the waitress snapped at us, and Hal slid back to his seat as she placed piles of food in front of us.

We ate in silence, the words sinking in. They kidnapped, maimed, and killed the only family this little girl had ever known, to have her hunt down more people they could use and abuse. What kind of sickos were they?

"And Charlie found them?" The rest of his conversation from earlier clicked into place.

"Yes, and when he calls, we will go there. Lucy will need you."

"Why do you sound like someone just told you they ate your puppy?" I reached across the table.

“Because putting you in danger goes against everything in me, and yet I can’t think of another way.” The rawness in his confession had so many emotions welling up inside me I couldn’t process them all.

“I don’t want anything to happen to you, either. I have plans for you later.” I attempted to lighten the mood only to sound like a sleaze ball propositioning someone at a bar.

“That works out well for me because I have plans, too.” He picked up his coffee and took a long sip. “It looks like I have less than a year to figure out what gift I need to put in that little bag.”

As awkward and weird as that sentence was, his words were perfect. Absolutely perfect.

Chapter Nineteen

The call came, and we were driving to the "medical" facility which was about a half hour away. His team was meeting us there, and while I had no clue what that would at all entail, it made me feel safer. If Lucy was recruiting, chances were I wasn't the first, and, adding into that the children they were brokering, there potentially could be a lot of children needing rescuing.

Gah, I wish I'd had more time with her, was able to find out more from her.

"So I am just going to drive up to the lab?"

"No. The directions are to the team. From there, we will await instructions.

And so meet the team we did. I had expected a ton of people, ranging from military types to paramedics. Instead, I was greeted with a group of four men and one woman.

"I expected…more," I confessed as I unbuckled my seatbelt.

"More is not always better. Our first goal is extraction, and that generally works better with fewer people."

"And if we need more?"

"Fear not, they are close by." He cracked his door open, effectively ending my conversation.

The next bit was a whirlwind. Charlie spoke over the earphones everyone, including me now, wore, giving us the layout of the lab based on old blueprints he had found and bunches of random information he thought might help us.

I, of course, was not to go inside unless and until they called me to do so. They wanted me at the ready to help with Lucy…period.

I didn't love that idea. In fact, I hated it, and I couldn't determine if my hatred was more because I didn't want her to have armed men wandering in and grabbing her, scaring her more than my familiar face would have, or if I was scared to be alone.

They walked me to where I needed to be and made me promise not to get up from my hidden position, not that being in the brush was a great hiding spot. They started toward where the lab was when Hal turned around, walked back to me, and squatted in front of me, pressing something on both his hat and mine. "Stay safe and don't do anything foolish." His hand cupped my cheek.

"I'm not. I promise." Of course, our definitions of stupid might be different, and I intended to do whatever I needed to save Lucy.

"By my definition."

I looked up at him, confused. I hadn't spoken those words. Had I?

"We will talk later about how you just did that."

"Promise there will be a later." It was such a ridiculous promise to ask for, but anyone who could murder then cover up said murder the way they did had to be far more dangerous than they appeared.

"I promise." He leaned in a kissed me softly on the lips, a kiss far too brief and chaste, yet somehow exactly perfect. "I can't miss our date." He kissed me again then pressed his hat and mine again and started mumbling about being on his way and them being jealous.

That kiss kept my mind occupied while I listened to their approach to the building, each of them taking their locations as directed by Charlie who somehow was watching things unfold from wherever he was.

Hal had kissed me and promised me our dream date. Not that I wanted it to happen like this. No, I wanted his eyesight to stay as functional as it was. It might be horrible, but as he said, in his memory, it was functional.

Slowly, the sounds of their voices, all except Hal's, faded away into the background, and it wasn't until I saw what I couldn't see that I put together that I was dreaming—awake and dreaming. How was that possible? I didn't even know I could do this.

Then my grandmother's words came back to me.

You know when it is time to share your secret.

I'd always taken those words at face value, but now I saw them for what they were. I was sharing my secret, my gift, with Hal, and not just by telling him about it or showing him things in our dreams, but literally giving him the power to use it as well. And somehow, we were doing all this while we were awake.

Oh Grams, why can't you be here to help me figure this all out?

He was in a side door, no one in sight, the lock opening with ease, thanks to some electronic doohickey Charlies had sent them all with. "I'm not leaving her without her," he promised—but not over the headphones. No he spoke in the dream state.

"I know."

He walked the corridor and through what felt like a maze, Charlie guiding him a lot of the way. It was eerie how few people he had to duck out of the way of. Shouldn't a medical research facility have a lot of employees? Except this wasn't a medical research facility, was it? It was all a front for a kidnapping and baby brokering scheme on a lever I couldn't even begin to fathom.

Hal clicked a door open using his keycard. It was dark, so very dark, and his vision made it even more challenging to discern what I was seeing. Down, down, down he went; one flight then two until he reached something I recognized.

“She’s there.” I spoke out loud, hoping it would transfer to him. “The scent is the same, the dampness the same. She’s there.”

“And here you are.” The man from the memory Lucy shared, the man who came looking for me, the man behind all of this.

I stumbled as I tried to get out of the brush, only to land on my ass and find myself face to face with a gun.

“Gene,” I said, needing to be sure and to show him I had a something over him which was either brilliant or stupid. I didn’t even know.

Everly.

Find her. I’m fine, I lied as I attempted to shut down our connection, fear overtaking me.

“Get up…slowly. I would hate to blow away the best find since the girl.”

I obeyed, unable to think of any plan better than to do so.

“My men will get rid of your little A Team wannabes, and then I will show you to your new room.”

A Team wannabes…he had no clue what he was

dealing with if he thought that was the case. I'd only met them briefly with the exception of Hal, and there was no part of me that didn't fully trust they were the best there was.

Please, just let them not be outnumbered.

"Why?" I asked, trying to buy time. "Why me?"

"As if you don't know." He threw a pair of handcuffs at my feet. "Put those on with your right hand and then press your front against that tree with your hands behind your back."

I slowly bent down, doing what he said and trying to decide whether he was afraid and that maybe I could overpower him, and that was why he had me leaning against the tree, or if it was simply because doing all this was just easier for him. The light was dim enough I couldn't tell for sure how strong he might be physically, and, since he held a gun in his hand, the point might be moot anyway.

He had me cuffed and getting in the back of a van I never heard enter the clearing. "Where are we going?" Because I needed to get my ass back to the lab.

"Turns out there is a little bit of trouble brewing. Your rebels are a little more skilled than I gave them credit for, so we are going to stay out of their way. Might as well sleep now while all your little friends are awake because you are not going to have any REM for as long as it takes to get you on board."

And then he let out the cackle, the one from my dream, and slammed the window separating us close.

I was good and fucked.

The only tool or weapon I had was being able to connect to Hal, and I wasn't even sure how this new facet of my ability worked. Would my getting into his mind prevent him from saving Lucy? If so, it wasn't worth it. She deserved a good life…she deserved a true childhood.

I closed my eyes and leaned back, not wanting to upset the crazy man with the gun. No one wants that.

We drove and drove over bumpy ground, and I found myself back in that space, the one Hal and I were sharing, only this time it was different. It seemed more real, as if I were standing with him.

There were all kinds of sirens going off and

confusion. All I could feel was confusion.

"Hal." I couldn't help myself, needing to hear him say he was alright, his emotions telling me he was anything but.

"Can't see. She's near. I can tell she's here." He glanced up, and I instantly saw why he was in such a frantic state. Smoke. There was so much smoke.

"Use my eyes," I called to him, praying he could. His comment about my eyes as his were useless at our dream dinner date gave me half an idea it was possible.

"How?" He then turned forward and called Lucy's name repeatedly.

I had no idea how. None. But I had to believe that if only I opened myself up enough, it could work. When he gasped and said for me to do it again, I knew I was on the right track.

I focused my entire energy into giving him my sight, something that, by any logic anywhere, was not possible. I nearly broke into tears as I felt his relief when he bent down and scooped up her far too still body. Or at least I thought it was hers. I couldn't see her or anyone else. As much as he was using my eyes,

I was using his. I forced down the panic building inside me. He needed to get her out of there and to some medical help.

Please, let her be okay.

The opening of the back doors yanked me from my state just as Hal filled his lungs with fresh air. They might not be out of danger, but he was away from the fire, and that was the best I could do for him.

"Out," Gene barked.

I scooched and slid out of the van and onto the dirt driveway. How long had we been driving? It felt short and long simultaneously. It didn't help that I was dancing between two planes.

He tugged a knit cap over my head, covering my eyes. "Can't have you seeing anything of value…you know, just in case."

From there, it was a short and stumbling distance until he barked at me to step up. One. Two. Three. Four steps.

""'Get in."

I heard a door open then he pushed me from behind, and I crashed on the ground.

"Get up."

"Not the way to keep me from a brain injury," I mumbled, my head pounding from how I landed.

I tried to get up and failed a few times.

"Get her up."

Oh shit, we weren't alone. Hands came under my armpits and helped me to my feet only to push me down again, this time onto a chair.

"The word?"

"Gone. It's gone." The man from the adoption agency's voice jolted me. Fuck. This was not good. It was very not good.

"Gene, we have a problem."

And sure as shit, as he kept talking, that problem was me. Next thing I knew I was being locked in a room, a jab slamming into my arm moments before being pushed down on a bed.

Staying awake was not an option, the drugs pulling me under quickly.

Hal. Was all I managed to get out before everything went dark.

There would be no dreaming.

Chapter Twenty

"She's waking up," a familiar-yet-not voice boomed in my ears.

"Loud." I reached up, covering my ears. Wait… I. Reached. Up. My hands were free. "What?"

I tried to crack my eyes, but they wouldn't budge. I tried again nothing. My head pounded louder than before.

"Don't try just yet, love." Hal—Hal was with me. His hand brushed my cheek. "You gave me a scare."

"Lucy?" I squeaked.

"Is fine. All of them are fine. Not Gene or our friendly neighborhood baby seller, they aren't fine. But everyone else is. I promise. Sleep, please."

They were fine. I was safe. Hal saved me…saved all of us.

"Stay?"

"There is no other place I would be."

The next thing I knew I was walking, the drugs had worn off at least that much. Compelled to run, I ran and ran and ran until I wound up in a room…no not a room. *Our* room. The one at the hotel. And Hal was waiting there for me.

"I hoped that if I waited long enough, you would show up."

This time, I ran into his waiting arms.

"You saved me, you know."

"Why do I feel that is my line?" I peppered his face with kisses, rich laughter flowing through me. We had both made it out alive, and the children were safe. What more could I ask for in life?

"We saved each other?" he compromised then his lips took mine, and, unlike the kiss we shared earlier, this one had us taking our time, letting the moment build as we explored each other's mouth.

When the kiss ended, both of us breathless, all I could manage to say was, "Wow!"

To which Hal replied, "Why do I feel that is my line?"

He held me close, and we stayed like that, just enjoying the feel of being in each other's arms.

"Mom," a little girl's voice echoed from the other

room.

“Do I…what’s going on?” I asked, already starting to piece things together. “Lucy?” She had written to her teacher, saying her new mom would find her. She was more than a walker. So much more.

“Is that okay?” Lucy came out wearing a princess costume paired with purple and gold beads, matching the clothing I found myself suddenly wearing. *Only in a dream.*

“I think I like it. I have to warn you though…you will have a brother who is very furry and not so good at listening.” I ducked down, opening my arms wide for her. “You have very pretty eyes.” I smiled, relieved that they were no longer sewn shut.

“They aren’t, not yet, but the doctor promises they will be tomorrow. I just didn’t want you scared of me…people are always scared of me.”

Her confession pierced me so deeply.

“You know my grams used to say people are scared of what they don’t know.”

“Are you mad that I went in your memory to learn?” she asked, and until then, I hadn’t thought much about it. "They hurt me when I didn't learn fast enough—that's why I found you."

"I am not mad. You needed to survive if I was going to find you. Probably best you don't do it anymore though." I stood up.

"I can't. Not really. Those were the only memories I ever saw…only one with your grams. I used to pretend she was mine, too, and that was why I could see her." She stepped closer and opened her arms, and I hugged her.

"She kind of is your grams now, too, isn't she?"

"I like that. Daddy says we have to do a ton of paperwork, but then you can really be mine."

I looked to Hal, and he half shrugged.. "Like you could say no to an offer like that." His huge smile was brighter than I'd ever seen.

"I gotta go." Lucy gave a wave. "I can hear the beeping in the background—some nurse is going to bug me soon." How was she so jolly at those words? She was there one blink then gone in the next.

"So how does this work? This *I am mom* and *you are dad* thing?" I asked, loving the sound of it. "I don't even know where you live."

"I live in hotels mostly. I can easily move near you."

"So this wasn't a ploy to get into my house and into my bed?" I sassed.

"Not that those aren't my long term goals, but no, it's not. And I did tell Lucy that straight-up. She said, and I quote, 'That's fine. You can wait until your wedding. And just so you know, the dress you picked out for me isn't princess enough.' Then she rolled her eyes. When did kids start doing that so young?"

"I'm sure your sister can tell you stories." I fell into his arms.

"You need to go get real sleep. The doctor is going to fix your eyes in the morning, and then we have things to do."

"Things?"

"Things. You know, moving, making sure all the people involved are either prosecuted or helped, and, apparently, we're getting hitched." He winked and then disappeared, the room fading away until all I was left with was a deep sleep.

Epilogue

One year later…

"Your eyes," he spoke wistfully, "They are so…amazing. Is that even the right words?"

I shrugged, cutting his steak, never sure how to respond to his compliments when it came to my sight, given he hardly had any of his own left. Not that he let it get in his way. He still did a lot of consulting for Phoenix Agency, working from home the way Charlie did—minus the mad scientist lair I discovered Charlie had in his basement the first time we went to visit him. The man had a way with technology, that was for sure.

"I guess." I finished cutting his steak then set the plate in front of him. "Steak at twelve."

It had taken Hal a while to accept that I wanted to help him and he was far from a burden. The fact he was the breadwinner, now that I was a full-time mama to our little girls, helped with that I was sure. Men are odd about such things.

It had been a no-brainer for me to stay home after

the adoption agency called saying they had found us a match. A thorough investigation proved that 95 percent of the agency was legit and that only a fraction had been shady—the fraction that Lucy's adoptive parents originally fell into.

Turned out they wanted to be her mother so badly, when finances fell through, they made a deal with the devil—their deaths a direct result of them trying to save her. There was an odd sort of comfort in that.

"Thanks, love." He set his fingers on the rim of the plate then trailed the tips to the left where he picked up his fork. "I always did love this place."

"Only because we had our first date here." I scooped a green bean onto my fork. "Although if I recall correctly, you insisted it wasn't a date." My tone rang with amusement.

"It wasn't. I was working." He pointed his fork in my direction to accentuate the point.

"If it wasn't a date, you wouldn't have bought me that beautiful dress," I countered. Of course, it was paired with fake wedding rings, but still. "No man buys a woman a fancy dress for a non-date. That's just ridiculous."

"I bought you the dress because you needed it." He shrugged. "But enough about that. When are you going to open your present?"

"Present?" I looked around then saw the small gift bag on the table.

"How quickly you forget. Maybe I should just keep it until our next anniversary." He chuckled, his voice deepening and oh so sexy.

"It's not our anniversary." Or was it?

"One year ago today was the first time I met you—or sort of met you." He put his fork down. "So present time."

I reached inside the small bag, and this time, instead of finding nothing, I found a small velvet box. My hand shook as I took it out and opened it. Tanzanite, low profile, just like I had randomly mentioned that day all those months ago.

I took it out of the box and flipped it to see if there was an inscription. Sure enough, there was.

For the woman of my dreams.

What more could I ever ask for?

Sign up for the Decadent Publishing Newsletter.

Where do you go when your life is in danger?

The Phoenix Agency

Titles in The Phoenix Agency by Desiree Holt

Jungle Inferno

Extrasensory

Scent of Danger

Freeze Frame

Feel the Heat

Formula for Danger

Unexpected Risk

Made in United States
Cleveland, OH
19 November 2025

26239974R10090